Demon Child

GRAYLIN FOX

Copyright

Demon Child
Copyright 2015 by Graylin Fox
Cover Art by Fiona Jayde

ISBN: 978-0-9966332-0-8

Arcane Court Novels

Death Dealer

Red Lady

Shadowed Vengeance

Novellas & Short Stories

Demon Child

The prologue is told from Cim's point of view. He's the dragon shifting lead character in the Arcane Court books. It was a blog post introducing Raye and Makenna published in 2014.

Prologue

"Cim, we have an emergency at the mall."

Grace took two steps at a time and was pacing in front of my desk before she finished speaking.

"The mall?" At six-and-half feet tall, I stood out in crowds. "I'd rather suck a demon tit."

She scoffed. "Look, dragon. There's a frightened demon child and we need to go get her."

"Ooh, rescuing kids. When did we start that business?" Wretch, the only born demon-dragon hybrid, chimed in.

Grace played the card guaranteed to win the fight. "Since Angie asked me to keep an eye on her."

"Tell us on the way." I grabbed my keys. My car sat in the garage at the back of the club.

If Angie had asked Grace to watch this girl, there must be a good reason.

My best friend was on his phone before we hit the street. "Demon teen, talk."

The shouting on the other end let me know someone demanded Wretch put his attitude up his ass with a thorny cactus.

"Have you ever helped a teen before?" Grace looked at me from the passenger seat as I drove.

"No." Our business model depicted demon decapitation. "Tell me about the girl."

She turned toward the window, her black hair hiding her face. "Angie worked with her mother at the hospital years ago. The woman is human and didn't know her husband was a demon until her daughter tried to claw her way out during a graveyard shift."

It explained how a human survived the birth. "Angie took pity on the woman?"

"They were friends before Angie met Uncle Fester back there." She gestured to Wretch. "Neither of them knew their boyfriends weren't human."

Angie's hand gun reaction to Wretch's demon shift during orgasm was legend in the local paranormal community.

"Who's the mom?" Wretch stuck his head over the seat. "Is she hot?"

A demon's demon. Complete with thousands of years of testosterone built in.

"She's hands off, Wretch." Grace pushed his face away.

I laughed. Good try, but if my best friend wanted to play, he would.

A crowd had gathered in the parking lot. I locked the car while Grace and Wretch began peeling off layers of demons.

"Excuse me? Who the fuck are you and what are you doing? There are sales going on!" I hoped it would work.

The pile began to diminish until it exposed a scared demon teen, currently appearing as the girl from The Exorcist and being held down by a human woman. A smattering of demons stood by cars pretending not to watch. This wasn't good.

"Wretch, clear the audience."

He grinned as he shifted from Ken doll with dark wavy blond hair with hazel eyes into a demon with horns, hooves, and random tufts of hair protruding from a slick pink hide.

"I can't believe women sleep with you." Grace stuck her finger in her mouth.

"By the dozens," he replied. His attempt to strut away got hindered by his hooves.

The human woman looked relieved to see us. "If I had known they looked like that, I wouldn't have married Ariel."

"You know us?" I raised an eyebrow.

"Angie gave me pictures of you. Told me to call for help if I needed it." She pulled the girl to her feet and with a look only moms have, made her shift back to human form. "I'm Raye. This is my daughter, Makenna."

"I'm Cimmerian, dragon shifter, also known as Death Dealer. This is Grace, a friend of Angie's; she's a jaguar shifter. The scary looking demon thing is Wretched Spawn. He's half-dragon, half-demon."

Grace shook hands with Raye, saying, "And all slut."

Raye laughed. "I'm familiar with the type."

The child's eyes were huge in her little head. "You're all different? Like me?"

I nodded. Kids weren't on my list of talents. I fought the urge to bow out with a made-up excuse.

Thankfully, Grace stepped in. "Yes, we're different. We need to get you out of here before the police show up."

Sirens in the distance didn't sound like they were headed our way. "I think we're okay for now."

"Can I please finish shopping?" The child looked distraught.

Dammit. "Are you okay?"

"My father said he'd show up for Christmas this year. I wanted to get him something he'd like."

She rocked back and forth on her lace-up boots. They matched the lacing on her jeans. A good look for a demon child. All in black, pale skin glowing through the ragged edges of pre-sliced jeans. Her waist-length black hair twisted into a rope-thick braid. A small tank top barely covered her blossoming breasts.

She looked me over. I had on jeans and a short-sleeved black sweater. Grace said it complimented my black hair and green eyes. As a dragon, my eyes became orange-red like fire. They stood out in the middle of deep purple scales and black wings. "Do I pass approval?"

Her blush covered her face. "Sorry, I've never seen other differents before."

"We're shifters," I corrected gently. She looked terrified. "It's okay. What are you getting your dad?"

Behind me, Wretch was threatening the gathered demons with pictures from his extensive surveillance network. It was good to have eyes everywhere.

"I want two gifts. If he shows up, a great watch. If he stands me up again, a certificate for castration." Her blue eyes lit up her small face.

"I like her." Wretch shifted back to demon dandy—linen slacks and a buttoned-down shirt opened modestly.

Her mother appreciated the new form. "I get Angie's attraction."

She was short, curvy, and would blend in with other women.

"Mom." The girl put her hands on her hips. One flip of her head and the black braid swung behind her.

"Ariel." Wretch spat the word out.

The mother, Raye, blanched. "What did you say?"

He looked over them at me. "Take the girl inside, I've got this."

Wretch and Raye eyed each other with suspicion. Ariel wasn't a demon name I recognized. Clearly, my partner knew him, by reputation if nothing else.

Grace glanced back and forth until she decided to stay with the mother. Great, a teen and I go shopping in a mall. It couldn't end well. I knew only one store owner. Hopefully, he'd be there in person tonight. He wouldn't miss a chance to sell.

"He knows my father." The girl walked, staring at her feet.

"It looks that way. How do you walk when you don't look up?" I kept an irritated growl from escaping my throat. It wasn't the girl that irked me, but a group of demons attacking a girl in the parking lot of a mall made me want to pull their limbs off.

She shrugged her small shoulders. "I can tell when there's something in front of me."

"Demon power. You want to stand out or try to blend in?"

"I blend in at school." She paused. "Normally. Today, everything is weird. I didn't know I'd shifted until some woman freaked out."

A small hand grabbed mine, the contact strange, to say the least.

Trying to be comforting, I squeezed it. "Humans fear us. Some of them can handle it, like your mom and Angie. Most, though, would lose their sanity if they found out."

She laughed. "Thank you."

"For what?"

"Being honest and not treating me like a kid."

"You have to grow up quick. Just remember, you'll be around to meet your classmates' great-grandchildren."

She jerked to a stop. "Really?"

No telling if she was scared or freaked out. "You okay with that?"

"Puberty, only one time?"

My turn to laugh. "Yeah, only once."

"Good." She shivered as I opened the door for her. "Let's get his over with, I hate the mall."

"I could clear the way."

"Human or dragon?" Big blue eyes begged me to shift.

I'd have to get her mother a copy of the Arcane Court laws. "Human form. No shifting in front of humans."

We headed for the jewelry store.

"Does my dad look like that other guy? With the horns and stuff?"

"I'm not sure what their natural look is. That form comes easier than all of the rest."

Wretch almost confirmed it once. Almost.

"So, I'm that gross?"

Trouble afoot. "No. You're half-human. That makes you different from them."

"Good." Her mood changed slightly, more confident.

We reached our destination.

Keith stood behind the counter in an empty store, the only one not teeming with people. He had a little shop on Bourbon Street but spent his time at the mall during the holidays. "Cim, can I get you another ring or necklace?"

"Not today. This is my friend, Makenna. She needs a watch worthy of her father."

Keith eyed her carefully, inhaling deeply. "Demon?"

"She's half-human. Dad has horns."

He leaned over the counter. "Do you like being part evil?"

Her hand shook in mine. "What did you call me?"

The shift began with her braid. It fell away in tatters as a scarred bald head appeared. I recognized the character before the claws grew. Freddy Krueger. She was good.

"Nice job on the quick change. Care to switch back so we can shop?"

Whatever reaction she expected, our non-response didn't hit the marl. Glancing around her, she looked through the open doors at the crowds gathered yards away. No one glanced at her. "What is happening?"

The shopkeeper shifted into a devilish form. "I'm a demon, too, child. The place is protected by magic. Cim would not bring a young one to a human store."

Her hand shifted to human; I felt the skin replace claws. She'd held onto me the entire time.

"If you can't control your shifts, you need to do business with other shifters and demons."

Wide-eyed with amazement, her response came through a nod.

Keith turned back into a dark-haired human. "Now, what did you have in mind?"

Careful to keep me close, she let go, searching the store. "I want to buy him a watch. One that can survive when he shifts."

"I like your taste," Keith said. He put four options on the glass case. "All of these will survive whatever he gets into."

I heard Wretch laugh before they entered, Raye and Grace on each arm.

"The stud still has it," Keith teased.

"We aren't available for him," Grace insisted, pulling away.

Raye left him behind to check on her daughter. "What did you find?"

"A store with a demon in it." The girl sounded more relaxed.

Her mother hugged her. "We'll find all sorts of places with shifters. I think school's the only place you should be around humans."

Makenna laughed. It was a beautiful sound.

They picked out a watch together and Keith waived the price. The walk back to the parking lot was quiet. No one spoke until we got to Raye's car.

"Thank you for coming." She held out her hand.

Shaking it, Wretch replied, "Any time you or Makenna needs us, you call the club and one of us will show up."

The girl fidgeted with her braid. "What if it's big trouble?"

I answered. "Then you'll get me, Wretch here, and George. He's really big and shifts into a gorilla. We might even bring a werewolf. We can handle anything that shows up, okay?"

Her smile lit up her face. "Okay. I'll be careful."

My convertible purred. I let down the top for the ride back to the club. Raye and Makenna needed to be added to our small list of families we watched.

"Anyone get her address?"

Wretch snorted. "And phone number and anything else you want."

My list was small. "That's Ariel's kid."

Grace turned to the back seat. "Spill it, Wretch. Who's Ariel?"

"One of the most dangerous demons around. No power base, no world-conquering ambitions. Just a vicious streak that cut a swatch of blood through a few major cities in the past century."

"And she's just like him." Her quick temper wasn't due to hormones, but genetics.

He sighed. "I noticed it. Maybe her mother's influence will calm down the sadistic streak."

"Get eyes on them tonight." I wasn't taking a chance. If Ariel was going to be here for the holidays, we needed to watch.

Grace interrupted our reminiscing with the most important information we'd learned. "Demons can have children with humans as long as the women are in hospitals for the birth."

I could see the hope in Wretch's eyes. The thing demons had given up on—mentally stable kids. Well, stable compared to pure demon.

It would be a Merry fucking Christmas this year.

The story of Demon Child begins now from Raye's point of view. It's close to the end of the school year.

Chapter One

I sat in the principal's office pretending it didn't bring back memories of my teen years. It was my daughter's turn in the hot seat. This time, she'd frightened an entire classroom. She's half demon and puberty wasn't going well. Instead of thirteen-year-old temper tantrums, my horror movie buff had shifted into Freddy Krueger, threatening her music teacher. My assurance that she wasn't as scary as her father didn't go over well, either.

Next to me, shifting in her chair, sat my only child. She was young, beautiful, and visibly terrified. I wanted to tell her it would be okay but they'd called her father and he'd either show up and charm the principal or burn the place down around us. Her long black ponytail frayed more as she twisted it in shaky fingers.

We waited.

"Hello, gorgeous," my ex-husband said, breezing through the door. "How can I help you ladies today?"

My daughter hadn't seen her father since she was five years old. She stared at him, then at me, then back at him. Yeah, I got that a lot. I stood five feet four inches tall, wore a size ten 'extra curvy' according to the helpful lady at the mall, with gray eyes and shoulder-length brown hair.

I could blend into the background anywhere. My ex-husband was stunning. He had long, wavy black hair that looked like silk, a body you see in the after pictures on infomercials, blue eyes, and enough charisma to bed an entire football stadium.

I coughed. "Hello, Ariel, nice to see you again. I have this covered."

Attempting to keep the fury from my tone turned it into a growl.

"Hello, Makenna," he said to our daughter. "Our child's in trouble at school," he added, reverting to me. I'm here to help."

Mrs. Adams, the stern principal who reminded me of the nuns from my childhood, just watched through irritated brown eyes, her brown, professionally highlighted hair twisted in a perfect bun.

"What do I call you?"

Makenna was mad. Her pupils changed to solid black.

"You can call me Dad," he said, kissing her hand.

Yanking her hand back, she rubbed it on her jeans. Her face scrunched up as she said, "How about dick weed? Jackass? Missing pieces? Sperm donor? Deadbeat asshole? Disney mermaid?"

I loved her. She'd been told, as soon as she was able to understand, about Ariel's gallant seduction. The fantastical dates where he took my heart, cell by cell.

Looking back, I recognized the glamour of demon magic weaving itself into me. I'd been entranced; it drew me in until the misty clouds of deception obscured the truth enough to get me pregnant, the fog lifting two days before I peed a plus sign on a stick.

At the time, I'd wished it stayed until I had Makenna. The truth of his manipulation sliced hope each day as pictures of his infidelity appeared online, on friends' phones.

The scents of other women wafted from him as he held my hair out of pregnancy barf. It still grated on my nerves.

"You call me Ariel," he said with a wicked grin.

"Like the mermaid," Mrs. Adams said under her breath.

"Yes, just like that," he replied.

With a flourish, he bent over and kissed her hand. For a moment, her eyes glazed over. The man could charm the pants off a Medusa frozen statue.

"Mrs. Adams, let me introduce you to my ex-husband, Ariel Gale. He sells real estate in the Caribbean. At least, that was his last known location and occupation."

Trying to keep the bitterness and anger from my voice made me spit the words through gritted teeth.

"My apologies for the animosity between my wife and myself," Ariel said, flexing his impressive arms. "Whatever my daughter did, I'm sure you can understand was due to the horrendous temper she inherited from myself and my family."

That was an understatement. When the judge had ordered him to pay child support and stay away from Makenna, he'd nearly decapitated the man. Instead, he'd waited until that night, materialized in my bedroom, looking like the cover model from the novel on my bedside table.

My refusal had caused a shifting frenzy that included mummies, vampires, the creature from Alien, and an extremely well-hung nun in a tattered habit. That one still showed up in my nightmares.

I grabbed my huge necklace in my right hand. It proved fashionable and heavy enough to knock a man out, or bruise whatever appendage he pointed in my direction. I wasn't skilled at fighting. I counted on luck to get me out of any danger.

The most I'd ever been in? Marriage to a demon stud. Oh, he'd never abused me, mentally or physically. Deception and magic were his tools.

"Let go of that stupid necklace, Raye."

He glared at me. I'd tested it's effectiveness on his nuts.

"Excuse me, Mrs. Gale. Can I see you in private?" Mrs. Adams indicated the hallway.

"Of course." I followed her out.

She fidgeted. This wasn't good. I'd never had to pull my daughter out of school. The possibility had lurked since her first outburst in daycare. She'd shifted in front of a mirror, scaring the class, but more important, she'd been terrified. Years passed before she gave into the urge again.

"Your daughter hates her father." Mrs. Adams looked stuck between attraction and revulsion.

I knew that feeling well.

"He left while I was pregnant, returning to fight for custody when she was days old. The battle lasted for four years. He knows a lot of lawyers, I'm sure he's related to a dozen." I'd told this story so many times. "Makenna's hurt for me and her. She feels he betrayed me."

"He's stunning." Her eyes glazed over.

"The pricks usually are."

She nodded absently.

"Makenna and I can handle Ariel. He breezes in and out every few years. I want to keep her in this school. She has great friends here and her grades are excellent."

All of my child support money went to tuition. Since Ariel owned the house we lived in, my nursing salary paid for food and clothes. With a new teenager, that still wasn't enough to keep up. I kept getting sidelong glares when we drove past classmates with the latest designer clothing.

"Your frequent donations to our alumni association have guaranteed Makenna's ongoing success here, Mrs. Gale." Her face lit up but nothing reached her eyes.

Without the donations, my daughter wouldn't be in this school.

It would be easier to hate him all of the time if I didn't know how much he loved his daughter. Which was why I loved it when she insulted him.

"I'll talk to her. I'm sure the horror movie marathons she's been watching are affecting her. Her first psychologist told me she would look up to male role models. My daughter picked the villains in movies because everyone feared them."

At least, that's the least creepy of the four things he'd said. I'll be forever grateful she didn't' shift at his office. I'm not sure she could've fought the anger at being locked up and the number of drugs they'd give her wouldn't have helped.

"Women wanted to be with them," the principal said mostly to herself.

"Do I need to pinch you?" She was a great advocate for Makenna. I'd like to keep her as an ally but if she started sleeping with Ariel, that would change.

Her hair didn't move as she shook her head.

"I'll be fine," she said to her shoes. "He did something to me, I don't feel right."

Chapter Two

Demon magic. He'd put the whammy on me a few times. I'd been meticulous about taking my birth control pills. Yet, I got pregnant. He wasn't surprised when I told him.

My pregnancy was supposed to end in a dungeon under an old plantation home owned by demons, with me dead and Makenna raised by her father. Only, I went into labor at work. The emergency room doctors yanked me into an open room. I wanted to deliver her naturally. If I had, I'd be dead. The movie Alien had to have been based on demon births. The children crawl out of their parents.

Demon mothers can shift to accommodate the gaping hole in their middle. Humans die during the first hour from blood loss. I'd flat-lined twice, the blank space in my memory a blessing.

My friends performed a cesarean section with my first curdling scream. The rest was a blur of IV fluids, drugs, and Ariel's voice sweet-talking in the background. A surgeon I'd dated a couple of times before I met Ariel stood up to him, physically forcing him outside of the intensive care unit as they rolled me in.

I regained full awareness three days later with my friend holding Makenna to my chest for feeding. She was beautiful and perfect.

Ariel's inability to get his daughter from me pissed him off. He vanished for months at a stretch even though New Orleans was his favorite city. During my maternity leave, all of the doctors and nurses present at Makenna's birth vanished.

I'd feared them dead until my surgeon friend sent me a letter saying he'd been offered a prestigious position at John's Hopkins. Ariel had struck again. At least, no one had died.

I'd fallen hard for him. Stunning, attentive, and I'd thought, devoted. I'm not much to look at. Now, I dated plenty—a sharp tongue and quick wit garnered attention.

Although, I don't stand out physically, my brown hair hanging nicely when I let it down, brown eyes clear and focused, and enough curves to hide the strength needed to flip a two-hundred-pound patient over in bed to change the sheets.

Ariel breezed through a club I was in with Angie. She'd been a great friend and the local coroner. We stood off to the side laughing about something and up he walked. We joked about his absurd ego and confidence from across the room.

So you'd think I would've turned him down when he asked me to dance. The place fell silent. Demon magic, I knew it now. At the time, the world around me stopped so I could sway with Ariel.

I'm pretty sure I'd fallen in love by the third song. How much of that was voluntary or magically assisted, I'll never know. The next morning I woke, prepared to find him gone, except he'd stayed and cooked breakfast. Even looking back, I understood why that had made me swoon.

I heard rumors about him before we dated. His ruthless reputation never fit in my mind with the kind, gentle, gorgeous man who treated me like a princess.

Over time, I felt a coldness creep between us. One I couldn't thaw and he wouldn't acknowledge. If I had known he was a demon at the time, the icy fog hovering over our bed would've made sense. As it was, I thought I'd lost my mind.

I'd denied it, of course. No woman wants to admit her husband's lying and cheating. My husband pleased an entire neighborhood before I threw him out. Then, I got angry looks from women who afterwards had to settle for their own husbands.

Knowing he stood on the other side of the door with our daughter made me antsy. I wanted to get back in there without being rude. Mrs. Adams didn't believe the students who told her Makenna looked like a monster. I wanted her to get this under control before one of the adults spotted her or she ended up all over social media.

One of the reasons I picked this school was their cell phone policy. They didn't allow them on campus. The kids could have the old flip phones for emergencies but the school administrator didn't want the students focused more on what to post than on their classwork.

We made it to the car without incident. Mak even got her books both from her classroom and locker before meeting me in the parking lot. She'd insisted I not follow her.

Wanting to tag along to prevent another shift would stress her and make it more likely, so I paced in the parking lot until she showed up, her father grinning like an idiot behind her. Wonderful, he shadowed her without her knowledge.

Uncomfortable silence filled with unasked questions and painful memories washed over us on the ride home.

Makenna said nothing as she stormed through the house heading to her room. It was her sanctuary. I wanted to run up and lecture her, mom-style, but I didn't. Ariel's reappearance rattled me. How did he find out about her shifting?

I'd hoped I'd get used to the different forms Mak shifted into when angry. I didn't.

Truth was, I feared her and she knew it. It said a lot about her respect for me that she didn't wake me in the middle of the night looking like a demon.

Something her father did once before I'd realized demons nuts also reside in the crotch. I'm a damn good kicker.

"Mom, I hate him." She stood with her hands on her hips at the top of the stairs.

"He's your father. I'm not going to give you the standard line and tell you he's okay and you're missing his good parts. You saw all of them on display today. However, he's a demon and I haven't experienced what you're going through.

I know there are female demons around New Orleans. Unfortunately, my friend who used to know who to trust isn't around anymore."

I loved Angie. She'd loved a demon-dragon shifter and his family had killed her for it. That added to my fear. I wanted to move away from the area but couldn't afford it.

"Angie was cool." She closed her door. I heard her favorite playlist thumping the walls.

Makenna's fascination with gore led to curiosity about the human body. When she was the coroner, Angie took Makenna to work.

I couldn't take her to the ER with me. She'd want to watch surgeries. My stomach turned at some of the things she found acceptable.

I fully expected my daughter to come back smelling like vomit. Instead, she loved it.

Ariel appeared in the living room. He paced back and forth, making growling noises.

"She's not a possession, you dick. You terrified the judge and lost custody. The three years you vanished was one hell of a temper tantrum. Do you know how often I had to answer a six and seven-year old's tear-filled questions about why her daddy didn't love her enough to visit? Women want to sleep with you, your daughter wants to decapitate you while you're sleeping. You might want to learn the difference."

"I talked to her principal." His grin told me he'd tried more.

"No, you spelled her principal and she knows you're scum. Not the demon part, but the slick prick part."

"You're still jealous." He preened.

I sighed. "Ariel, I stopped being jealous of you after you hit on all of my friends. When they turned you down, I started to see the man behind the flamboyant romantic. You're vicious and cruel. Makenna may never want to be a part of your life. She has that choice."

If he took her away from me, I'd have to call in favors I'd made with a friend. It would be ugly.

"She can choose after she's seen what I can offer. Trips around the world, cruises with celebrities, unending power and money. Even if I wait until you die, Raye, I'll have her for centuries."

He knew where to hit me.

My influence with my daughter would end in less than a decade. I'm her mother and she'd grow up and, likely, move away. She doesn't like the high concentration of demons and shifters in New Orleans.

Pretending to be human doesn't work with other paranormals around. She wanted to move to Iowa or some other place full of land and wheat and corn, things that would bore me to madness.

"Her fury at you may last millennia. Ever think of it that way? You got her mother pregnant, knowing and hoping that giving birth would kill her. She loves me, Ariel. Even after she finishes mourning my death, you may be on her grudge list. Demons keep those handy, don't they?"

He'd explained, once I'd found out about demons, that they carried grudges for lifetimes. It's like playing an eternal game of high school grudge match.

My stomach growled. "I need food. Leave her be. She knows where to find you if she wants. She still has the contact spell. I've never prevented her from contacting you."

Expecting him to challenge me, I pulled my shoulders back as I left the room. He owned the house. Hating that fact didn't change my indebtedness to his boundless fortune. He'd stolen gold from a dragon centuries ago and invested it well.

Dragons—another group I didn't want to know. Yet, the local law enforcement for New Orleans seemed decent enough.

Cim, the dragon shifter, and Wretch, his business partner, gave us their numbers. Just in case. I hoped we wouldn't need it today. Their reactions last December when Wretch realized she's Ariel's daughter. I shivered. There was a history there.

"Ariel. Please leave," my daughter yelled from the back of the house.

"She knows my name."

"It's not Dad," I poked, pushing through the swinging kitchen door.

He caught it behind me. "It's a start."

I sighed. "She shifted into a horror movie character in class. She's not proud of that. Unlike you, I'm sure you'd take a picture and send it to your friends."

"I'm over two thousand years old, I don't do social media." He tilted his head when he thought. "Would I find pictures of her on the internet?"

"Probably, on her friends' pages and accounts. It seems this new generation can't speak face to face. I limited her to texting and talking on her phone. Lucky for us, she doesn't want her pictures out there." For that, I was grateful.

"You aren't yelling at me."

"Hating you is a waste of my time. I have a daughter to raise." I found my hands on my hips like a middle-aged Peter Pan.

"You're scowling at me."

"And?"

"You know I loved you once," he said.

"Never as much as you loved yourself."

"Well, duh."

Makenna walked in from the hallway. She'd clearly been listening. "Spoken like a true ditz. Why are you here, sperm-donor?"

"I was in the area."

Her eye roll included a full head turn. "The truth would be nice."

Caught off guard by his daughter's calm doubt, Ariel looked confused. "But I was."

Her hand smacked the middle of his chest, slamming him into the wall. The room shook.

"Try again. I've taken every form of martial arts to learn how to control the anger you gave me. I'd love to demonstrate how to decapitate a demon in under five minutes. Wretch is a very good teacher."

I'd seen her angry before; this was fury.

The room filled with a fog. Beyond my ability to handle this, I reached for the phone. Over Makenna's head, Ariel mouthed 'no.' He looked scared. Good. I held my fingers over the numbers.

He didn't fight back. "Do your worst."

It was a statement, not a challenge.

A distinction I clearly heard. She didn't. Twelve-year-old hormones combined with bullies picking on her had the demon side of her infuriated. I knew she couldn't beat him. Hoping he loved her enough not to kill her wouldn't work, either.

I tapped at her shoulder. "He's not trying to kill you, Mak, and he could."

If keeping my daughter alive meant kissing his ass, I'd buy the lip-gloss.

"I could kill him, Mom. I know I could." She spoke with calm confidence.

Even Ariel's eyes grew at her statement. "You'd have to take my head off."

"I know." She shifted into a demon form I'd never seen on her.

It frightened me. "Mak?"

"I'm fine, Mom."

It was meant to calm me. Instead, the gruff fury in her voice froze me in place.

For the first time since he'd left me, I looked to Ariel for help. His eyes wide, he didn't glance away from her. It was the second time I'd seen him scared.

I'd nearly been hit by a car while pregnant. He'd murdered the driver that night, after the police and bystanders had laughed about him panicking over a near miss at barely twenty miles per hour.

Ariel's breathing slowed.

"Mak, don't kill him." She'd never forgive herself.

"Why the fuck not?"

"Okay, grounding you for the cuss words, again. Now, shift back to something less disgusting and let your father go. He's not breathing," I said between ragged breaths.

Her grunt startled me as she shifted back to human, dropping Ariel. He slid to the floor, holding his neck with both hands.

"She was going to kill me." Centuries of arrogance fell away, leaving fear of his child distorting his beautiful features.

"Don't talk about me like I'm not here. I've been here, in this house, every day of my life. Where have you been? Or, more accurately, who have you been doing?"

I'd never discussed her father's slutty ways with Mak. It seems I didn't have to. "Mak, go easy on him. He was jumping from bed to bed for centuries before I met him. It was crazy of me to expect him to stop."

You'd have thought I'd fluffed his nuts the way he preened.

She didn't buy it. "He married you. That should've meant something."

Watching him deflate fascinated me. The years of fights we'd had rushed back, only this time, it was my daughters' voice. He didn't argue with her.

"You are right, Makenna. I should've stayed," he said.

I fought to keep my chin from smacking the hardwood floor. "Why now?"

He sighed. "I got a call right after Christmas. The attack in the mall parking lot. You couldn't call me?"

"Why? Would my imminent demise bring you running?" Bitter? Yes, I was. "Cim and Wretch handled it. They've kept an eye on us. We're covered, Ariel, by two men who keep their word."

He rolled his shoulders back. Mak stepped between us, eyeing him in that defiant teenage way. It hurt him.

As happy as watching him in pain made me, I needed it to stop before I started to feel sorry for him. "Mak, he won't hurt me. He needs me to raise you."

"Not anymore," he whispered.

The words clanged around in my head like storm sirens. The room felt foggy and I grasped the wall to keep from falling over.

Makenna didn't budge. "I need her. I don't need you. Get out of my house."

"I own this house. Who do you think pays the bills? Your mother? Being a nurse doesn't make the bills, much less the mortgage. I set up the account that covers your every wish." He spat.

She turned to me. "Christmas?"

"All out of my check. I have a separate account," I assured her.

A nod of thanks from her preceded a fist to her father's throat. "Leave, or kill me in a fight."

He vanished.

Stunned, I didn't move.

"Mom, are you okay?" She was my little girl again. "I didn't scare you, did I?"

"In the best way," I said, hugging her. "That man still takes my breath away but now it's fear, not love."

"He used you to get a hybrid daughter?"

"You got that part, huh?"

I texted Cimmerian, the local Arcane Court law enforcement for paranormals, to tell him Ariel had shown up. His network would keep track of him. They couldn't save me if Ariel killed me in my home. I didn't allow them in the door. But if her father showed up at her school or followed her home, he'd get a beating.

"Seeing his face when I hit him felt good, Mommy," she said, looking like my baby girl again. "I know that's wrong."

"You're part demon, Mak. What's right and wrong will be confusing. Human rules really don't apply. We can do this but you have to stop shifting during class. There are kids at your school who go to the shooting range for fun. What's going to happen when they shoot you and you laugh?"

"They'll stop shooting me."

She had me there.

"Only long enough to get bigger weapons. You can't do that," I said, fighting back tears.

She rolled her eyes in that classic teen girl move. "Mooom, I'll be fine."

"I can't help you through this, Mak. It's so far out of my experience. I'm frightened for you, for us."

"Is there anyone who can help me?" She wrapped her arms around me.

"Let me ask around. There has to be a female demon in the area we can trust."

I couldn't believe I'd said that out loud, much less hoped it proved true.

A text came from Cimmerian—they'd keep an eye out for Ariel. I replied asking for names to help Mak through her transition. He said he'd get back to me.

Mak brewed her tea while I make a huge cup of coffee for myself.

"You're missing the rest of the day at school. Make sure you call someone to get the assignments and notes." My mom switch never turned off.

Her groan filled the air. "Even mid-crisis, you remember homework."

"It's a gift."

We walked to the back porch. The backyard was my sanctuary. The front was all Ariel. Old world-style furniture, heavy carved couches, and chairs made it look like a museum in a castle.

Out here, I'd put in a koi pond, rows of roses, orange and pear trees, and three separate seating areas surrounded by flowers.

Mak made her way to the rocking chair by the magnolia tree. I sat there with her when she was an infant. The smell of the blooming flowers eased the tension from my shoulders.

My work schedule was three days on, four days off. Since Mak only lost it on my days off, I had to wonder how much control she had.

The phone rang. "Hello?"

"Raye, nice to speak with you." It was Wretch, Cimmerian's best friend and a demon hybrid himself.

"Why do I feel like I need a shower?" I asked.

He laughed, a nice sound. His physical beauty hid a darkly dangerous demon.

"Give your daughter my mother's phone number." He recited it for me. "She can answer any questions and even stop by if you need her to. Also, send her by twice a week now for fighting lessons. I want you to come with her. She needs to know how to defend herself against other demons and it couldn't hurt to teach you, as well."

"Thank you." My shoulders slumped in relief.

He hung up.

Mak stared at me.

"Wretch's mom is in the area. He's going to teach both of us to fight demons. You now go twice a week, with me along." I gave her the number.

Her shoulders drooped. "Thanks. I don't want to be trouble. When I try to keep my feelings in, it burns. Like I've swallowed fire."

"You can go inside and call her, I'll stay out here."

She kissed my forehead before running inside.

Ariel appeared in front of me. "I approve."

"I don't give a fuck what you think."

He blinked. "I'm aware of that but you can't handle this."

"I know. I wouldn't have to if her father had a decent bone in his deceitful body. You could've kept in touch with her. The judge said you weren't reliable enough to raise her; there's never been a restraining order."

Secretly, I'd been thrilled he wasn't around.

He sat where she'd been minutes before. "I left because I wanted her to have a human childhood. Demons familiar with the layout of this house can appear in it, at any time."

I almost gagged on my coffee. "You expect me to believe you left because it was best for our daughter? You stomped out of the custody hearing while our daughter screamed for you to come back. You shattered her heart that day. It may not be fixable."

"No, I don't expect you to ever believe me."

Believing him meant opening myself up to that pain again. I fought it. Years went by before I'd let another man touch me. Even then, I'd screamed part way through. He'd never called again. I'd been celibate since. Makenna came first. Trying to explain to a new man that your daughter was a demon couldn't have ended well, so I didn't try. Ariel didn't kill me in childbirth but my dating life died the day I met him.

"You never remarried," Ariel said, trying to look casual.

"Nor did you." As far as I'd heard.

His face twisted into a bewildered expression. It looked painful. "You ruined my playboy reputation. Every demon or shifter I played with knew about you and Mak. I have no idea how you did it. Even overseas, women looked at me like I'm scum."

There was a silver lining to his showing back up. "Can't say I'm sorry to hear that."

"I thought you'd like it. I'll be in town. If you need me, call."

He was gone before his words faded.

His Drakkar cologne hung in the air. I'd thought it was the best smell when we'd met. Until I found out he, and other demons, used it to cover their stench. The real smell crept up during sex one night. I'd barfed all over him.

Laughing at the memory, I went inside to find Mak taking pages of notes in the kitchen, her schoolbooks spread over the table. I nodded, making another cup, and then going up to my room.

The wedding album slid out from under my bed with ease. Sealed in plastic, I'd closed it before Mak arrived. The pain ripped through my memory.

Ariel's presence lit my life while he'd been at my side. Our wedding day made the papers. His gorgeous face smiling for the cameras as I looked at him with all the love I knew how to give.

I'd stared at that picture for weeks after he'd left, dissecting it. I'd decided he stared ahead to check for other options while I only watched him. His seductive style at the school reminded me that he'd seduce a chair if he thought it would fondle his nuts.

Mak needed her father right now. It burned me to admit it. I wasn't simply ill equipped to handle her, I set her off. Mother and daughter, we'd grown up together. I'd been twenty-two and naive when she came into this world ripping my body open and demanding her due.

The picture section in her baby book missed delivery day. The gruesome aftermath scrawled across my abdomen in ragged scar tissue. Hidden from the world by one-piece suits and large panties, I protected her from herself. I couldn't do that any longer. I needed a demon's knowledge and power to pull her away from situations where she might hurt others.

The parking lot at the mall flashed in my memory. Without intervention, we'd have been dead. Even the youngest demon that evening had had centuries on me. Cim and Wretch had showed up, just like Angie said they would.

Choking back tears, I ripped the plastic wrap from the cushioned book, my hands caressing the tiny pearls sewn into the cover.

"It was the happiest day of my life."

I heard the pain in his voice as he appeared next to me. Torturing must've been on his to-do list.

I breathed deep. "I don't believe you. You got me pregnant to further your family line."

There, I'd said it. Out loud to him for the first time. He knew I knew.

I waited for the practiced denial and syrupy sweet explanation about how I should be grateful he took the extra step of marrying me.

"Raye, you believe that?"

His question rocked me.

Seeing his face would melt my resolve, so I straightened my back. "Yes. I've known it since I came out of the hospital. Humans don't survive demon births. Angie told me that while I was pregnant. Of course, I didn't believe her. Your words still wound around my heart, making me hope we'd be a family."

"I'm back now," he whispered.

Rustling of clothes warned me he'd moved closer. I set my jaw.

"Stay back." I noted he hadn't denied it.

"My love, Mak needs me now. Her shifts will become stronger and more frequent. You can't send her back to that school. If she kills a human, I can't save her."

At least, he wasn't slinging spells at my mind.

"Of course you can, she's a child." I wouldn't fall for his act even if he did sound genuinely worried. His concern for her felt genuine.

"The Arcane Court laws govern all paranormals. No human deaths. Period. The punishment is decapitation. Cim and Wretch would take me out themselves if I harmed you."

It says a lot about my mental state that suicide-by-demon crossed my mind. Mak needed one of us to protect her, no matter how strong and scary.

For a brief moment, though, I considered no parents as preferable to Ariel alone.

I swung my head around, frustrated that he'd been contacted. It was Mak's Christmas shopping trip where she'd bought a watch for him. It sat wrapped in her room since he'd not shown up. Mak had saved her allowance for it. The first time she'd done that for him, and likely, the last.

He took a step back. "They called me, Raye. She's on the local Demon Lord's radar. Kragen is a drug dealer. His morals make me look like a nun. If she messes up, his anger at me might keep her alive as leverage, but it's doubtful. Most demons don't survive their first century. We're lousy parents."

"Husbands, friends..." I could go on.

"Okay, you got me. I bolted. I'm a horrible husband and father. Kick me in the nuts every day as long as you let me guide our child through puberty. It will get worse, Raye. She hasn't turned into her true demon form yet."

Fear flashed through me. I knew it showed on my face.

He sat on the floor next to me. "We look like giant bats with horns, tufts of hair growing in no pattern at all, clawed feet, bony hands at the end of wings with talons, and we stink. You know about the smell part. Our skin is a slick, pink rubbery mess."

"So you pick human forms that look like cover models?" I asked.

"Can you blame us?"

"It's false advertising. I walked down the aisle with the body I see in front of me, not the disgusting creature you are."

His face fell. "You mean my real form?"

"Uh, yeah. That one. Makenna looks like that?" My pretty girl hid a monstrous figure beneath her wavering control?

He reached for my hand. I pulled the wedding album between us.

Ariel sighed. "I disappeared so she could have a normal childhood. Look, I fought for custody because I wanted to take her away, somewhere she could be raised by demons. You won the legal battle. If we'd never gotten married, it wouldn't have cost me four years in court."

He looked angry again. "She's my first child, my only child. I'm not going to lie and tell you I was faithful. As soon as you filed the divorce papers, I signed them, giving you a full bank account, that I still load up every month, the house I'd lived in for fifty years, and anything else your damned lawyer demanded."

"Yet, you fought for years to pull my daughter away from me." It still infuriated me.

"Raye, I married you. I'm practically immortal. You'll live eighty to ninety years, and I pledged myself to you."

"Until death, Ari. Not until your penis had an urge for a brunette with gravity-defying tits on Bourbon Street."

A sharp intake of breath. "You knew?"

If I could've shot daggers with my eyes, his face would've been unrecognizable. "You made the news. While I sat home, barfing at food commercials, you played in front of television cameras."

He stood up.

"Walking away again?" It shouldn't hurt. I yelled inside my head, *you're supposed to be over this already.*

Instead, he pulled me to my feet and into a hug. The kind of death grip hug only a demon or shifter doles out. Part supportive but deadly within seconds, if necessary.

"You're stiff."

"You expected me to throw myself at you?"

"I'd hoped." His grin could melt glaciers.

"Get over it, Dad. You're not her kind of monster." Mak stood in the doorway, smirking beneath happy eyes.

"He's not a monster," I protested, weakly.

"Mom, I get it. We aren't evil, well, not completely evil. Demons do kill humans, by the shit loads." She purposely looked at her father to ignore my scowling at her language. "I'm a demon. The creatures special effects shops pretend they've seen so they can create them for movies."

"Mak, most special effects artists are demons." Ariel loosed his grip from hostage to captive. "They intentionally don't put our true form on screen."

"Because, barfing," she snapped, shifting to a hairless wolf on two legs.

Ariel looked over the form. "You missed the sex organs."

"No, I left them out on purpose. It's my favorite change. I can avoid entrance holes as long as possible."

You know that moment you realize your child listened to you, only got the message wrong? That was mine. All the ranting of a woman, celibate by choice, who needed love and sex. Mak heard it all. Her take away was to shift her female parts closed. There was a tiny pleased voice telling me she wouldn't get pregnant as a teen. Still…

The arms around me flinched as I grasped them for support. Her father's exhalation blew my hair back.

"What?" My ragged voice came out as a whisper in the room.

Makenna shifted back to human-looking like we'd caught her with a boyfriend. "I don't want to have sex. Ever. So, I shift my parts closed."

Her long black braid smacked the door frame as she whirled around.

I shivered involuntary as her form retreated to her room. "Ari, I didn't know you could do that."

"I'm not the celibacy parent." He looked mortified.

The irony hit me as I attempted to process the last few hours. Choking sounds accompanied my attempt at sarcastic laughter. Exhaustion hit me as I lowered myself to the floor. Three twelve-hour shifts over the weekend bumped into Mondays. I'd asked Mak to keep that one day of the week calm, if possible. My brain wouldn't stop spinning for another few hours.

I needed rest. "I still won't keep her from you."

"I know." He stared at the door his daughter had walked through.

We could hear music in her room. Other than the shifting, she was a normal tween born to a single mom whose dad took off. Many of her classmates had one parent or another out of the picture. I'd ranted about it to my friend Angie.

As pissed as I was at Ariel, I had questions only a demon could answer. "I can't do this, Ari. The whole shifting thing, I don't understand. It appears instinctual. She's fine with the shifts even if it scares her classmates."

"It's a part of who she is. The human side of her will cease to be over the next two years. If she'd been part shifter, it would be different. Human genetics aren't strong enough to withstand demon." He almost sounded apologetic.

I wanted to stay angry at him. "Who are you and what have you done with the asshole I married?"

He coughed to cover his laugh. "When I got the message that you and Mak were attacked in the mall parking lot, I felt horrible. I should've been there to protect you."

"You've missed more than one opportunity to step up." One guilt trip doesn't make a parent.

He glared at me. "I've been a prick for centuries."

Like he was proud of it. "You should've said that on our first date."

"I think I did." He took my hand, rubbing between my thumb and forefinger.

"I haven't been able to date." Okay, I knew I was whining but it's a big deal to play happy celibate parent when hot men walked around without shirts.

"How long?" he asked.

Long enough for me to consider having sex with him. "Frustrated doesn't cover it."

"You want?" His face lit up with naked desire.

Unfortunately, I couldn't forget who he was long enough to play with his body. "Ariel, I'm fully functional. Casual sex was never my style."

"I know, I had to marry you." He grumbled.

I tried not to laugh in his face, turning my head slightly. "Any serious relationship would have to include Makenna's species. I'm not sure how to explain that to relatives who already love me, much less a new guy looking to make a good impression."

"Mom."

Oh, shit, she'd heard me.

"Yes, honey?" I turned to see her pale in the doorway.

"You're alone because of me?"

There was no denying it. I'd never lied to her and I wasn't starting now. "I blame your father."

He gasped trying to spout a snappy comeback.

I laughed, hard.

Makenna, still looking more worried than a child should, sat down next to me and took my hands. "I'll leave. You deserve to be happy."

I brushed her hair back from her eyes. "With you, I am."

Her father turned to us looking left out. "I suck."

"Yes, you do." She didn't miss a beat. That's my girl. "But Mom hasn't thrown you out yet, so she's not afraid you'll hurt us."

"Physically," Ariel and I said simultaneously.

His sigh filled the room with the smell of coffee. Ariel's biggest vice. He would spend hours at coffee shops talking to anyone who walked in. We'd spent many dates getting to know each other while trying different flavors.

When I'd mentioned falling for him to Angie, she'd gone ghost white, pulling me aside to tell me he was a demon. I didn't believe her and was too in love to let news like that stand between me and a hot guy.

If I'd listened, I'd be married to a nice human guy and have a life full of carpooling, soccer, and girl scouts. Instead, I sleep safe knowing my daughter can kill intruders before fully awake.

She ran to her room, returning with a notebook and pen. "Then I need to know everything about you. That way, I can find you when you take off."

"If, not when," Ariel said.

I eyed him. Makenna didn't change her statement; just sat there waiting for him to talk.

He cleared his throat. "I'm over two thousand years old. My mother and father were both demons. They left me in a small village in what is now Sweden, along the border with Norway. Demons parents don't do more than make sure you arrive safely into the world. The rest is shaky. It's no wonder we have no compassion. It's not a virtue we experience."

Mak glared at him. "No making it look fluffy."

Ariel sighed, his shoulders bending under the weight of his daughter's glare. "It was brutal. We're not a friendly species. Fighting for dominance with dragons, who used to be the size of airplanes, made us more vicious. Using humans to search for dragon lairs, test new spells, and to breed with demons got folded into our culture so slowly we'd never thought about the level of brutality. It's survival. Humans are our lab rats."

My daughter rolled her eyes.

He looked exhausted. Obviously, he'd never spent much time around teens. I covered my mouth with my hand to hide a smile.

"We killed thousands. Before plumbing, before electricity..." He looked up as Mak gasped.

"No power?" she asked.

A genuine laugh rumbled from Ariel. I hadn't heard that sound since I'd told him I was pregnant. "No computers, cars, light bulbs, stoves, refrigerators... you get the idea."

She shivered. "Still."

"Yeah." He sat silent. "You have to keep from shifting at school. Your classmates will be frightened but they aren't the threat. The group of demons who came after you at the mall are my enemies. If they find you, they'll kill you to make me suffer. I'm not a nice man, Makenna. You know that. I've made some serious enemies and now, they know killing you would hurt me."

A semi truck of pain slammed into my chest, sending waves of pain through my body while whooshing all of my air across the room. I opened my mouth wide, sucking in breath. "They're coming for my baby girl?"

He nodded. "I checked around before showing up. If it had been random demons scaring shoppers at the mall, I wouldn't be here. One of them works for the local Demon Lord. It could get deadly."

"That was over the holidays. You couldn't call to tell me? The school year is almost up. What took you so long?" I asked with a growl.

Mak slowly lowered herself to the floor. I was proud of her, I'd have passed out. As it was, I fought hard to breathe while colors floated behind my eyes.

Ariel opened his mouth to speak. No words came out. I saw pain in his eyes. It didn't fit with his human form. The gorgeous face he created each day twisted as he fought to find words.

Mak intervened.

"I'm a target. Wretch told me it would happen." She glared at her father. "Because of who you've worked for. I wanted him to be wrong. Seems you need to kiss some demon ass while I figure out how to survive your past."

The stare she gave him narrowed as her pupils grew. All trace of white disappeared and took with it the illusion she was human. Sour sweat smells filled my nose. The demon, whom I loved and would die for, emerged. Frightened for her, and myself, I grappled with the right words to say, finding all of them slipping through my shaking mental fingers.

Her father reached out a hand, shifting as he did so, and cupped her leathery, sickly pink cheek in his claw.

"I'll save you from Kragen. He doesn't win this one." The determination in his voice sounded bolstered by the gritty texture present from the shift. "You've been training with Wretch for months now. I'd rather you didn't need to use those skills in battle just yet. However, if they show up here, shift to your natural form and get between them and your mother. To rip my heart out, they'll start with breaking yours."

I'm pretty sure passing out wasn't the sexiest thing I could do. The hallway whirled as I heard my head thunk on the floor. My last thought was hoping I didn't bleed on the hardwood. I'd polished it the day before.

Chapter Three

I awoke to ice water rolling down my cleavage. Shivering, I pushed away the wash rag, knocking loose an ice chip which landed on my collarbone. Memory slammed into me as I feared Ariel had taken my daughter.

"Mak," I shouted.

"Sh, mom. I'm right here." She ran the cloth over my forehead. "Dad's making phone calls in the kitchen."

"Doesn't that make you less safe?" My throat clenched.

Her sigh conveyed exasperation for the poor, ignorant human. "I'm a demon. Hard to kill."

That didn't help me at all. "Mak, you're a kid. Even with demon magic, you can't stand up to beings centuries old."

"Millennia," Ariel said. I heard his feet on the area rug.

Blurry figures vaguely resembling my daughter and her father loomed over me. Blinking didn't clear the fog. An ache poked at the base of my skull, warning of the coming migraine's severity. I'd soon be mewling in oblivion, shivering in cold darkness until it passed.

Opening my eyes caused my breakfast to lurch. I closed them again. "You say the sweetest things."

"Caustic words will get you everywhere." He practically purred.

I heard Mak's gagging sounds. "Ew. Stop."

"We're your parents. Making you squicky is our job," I said. Forcing myself to sit up, I opened my eyes cautiously. The stomach revolt quelled. "We need to get you to safety. Ariel, I know you have safe houses around the world. Where can you put us?"

His lips formed a slit, anger filling his eyes. "You can't go. Makenna could get through the magical barriers, I hope."

"You hope?" She asked him.

He twitched. "They're built for demons. You're half-human." He waved a dismissive hand at me. "I can't hide you away. Demon magic can find hybrids from miles away. We'd be found before we knew we were in danger. You need to be protected."

My daughter curled up in the curve of my arm. "I'm safer with Mom."

Much to my surprise, Ariel nodded in agreement. "Yes, as I've said for years. My skill set is seduction and theft, not protection. I've talked to Wretch and Cimmerian. Wretch's mother, Iona, one of the eldest demons, is willing to keep an eye on you until Kragen tires of threatening me and moves on."

"I called her earlier, she sounds nice," Makenna said.

"What makes you think he will do that?" Hope dared to flicker in my gut, quelling the building pain nausea.

Ariel sighed. "He's the local Demon Lord and on the Arcane Court. If he violates any of the Court's laws now, he'll be decapitated on sight."

A slight chuckle fell from his lips. "Ironically, Raye, your humanity will save both of you. Human protection, and ignorance of our existence, is one of the main rules of the Court. If Kragen, or any of his associates, kills or uses you for a toy, their heads will roll."

"Into ash," Makenna whispered, grasping the severity of the situation. Her shoulders shook with fear as her fingernails dug into my side.

"Our daughter is half-human. Does that protect her?" I asked.

Ariel's eyebrows shot up. "I think it does."

He took off to the kitchen at a jog.

"I hope he's right," I said.

Mak's face scrunched up. "You still love him."

Gritting my teeth, I forced the words out. "I want to rip his heart out and watch him shift until he builds a new one. Then do it again, and again, and again."

She snorted. "Oh yeah, you got it bad."

I'd wondered myself if he could still tempt me. "*Had* it bad. If you didn't need him, I'd kill him myself."

"He married you, Mom." Her hands rested on her hips in an unconscious mimic of the way I looked when we fought.

"Are we doing this again now, Mak?"

Like any little girl who grew up dreaming of her daddy, Mak vacillated between hatred and adoration. Venomous in her anger and unrelentingly wistful in her hope that I'd been wrong about him. We'd fought a few years ago, for weeks, when the ridicule of nasty classmates trailed her home from the father-daughter dance.

A doctor friend had escorted her. The drastic contrast between her thin, pale frame almost hidden by sheaths of black hair and his tanned, natural glow, powerful build, and smiling blue eyes peaking from unruly blond hair had been stark, to say the least.

Standing in for Ariel had been Sam's idea, after he'd heard me distraught on the phone trying to get Ariel to show up for one night. I'd spoken to six women and none of them had passed him the phone.

His mocking laughter had lit a furious torch in me, which I'd used to fuel words of hatred spewed at the last woman to hold the phone. I'd loved my old wall phone that night—I'd slammed it down so hard it had tilted forward.

"Yes, Mom, because he's here."

"Until we're safe. Then, he's off playing footsie with every set of boobs in town." For the past seven years, I'd saved money to break free. There was enough to fly to the Caribbean. Demons can't swim, a chink in their armor.

"How do you play footsie with boobs? Do you have to wash your feet first? Oil up the tits and get a pedicure at the same time?" She leaned forward to catch my glare. "Really, what do you think the internet is full of, Mom? Cats?"

My mother had told me there'd be a day I'd want to melt into the floor out of embarrassment.

Mak rolled her eyes and sighed with all the inner angst only a tween could manage.

"There are things online I will never know how to do. You shouldn't be looking at those."

She smiled, a devious glint in her eyes. "Sure, you write down the list of sexual positions and things you've done and I promise not to look them up."

Twelve, she was twelve years old and talking the way I did in my twenties. I'd panicked at first. Her sexual education class at school had real sex information. One of my coworkers, a pretty young nurse barely out of school, had tried to keep the pity out of her eyes when she'd told me the internet took the mystery out of sex. It also made it look far more vulgar, nasty, and disgusting. So, Mak's curiosity might make her less likely to start experimenting early, she assured me.

I'd prayed that night for the first time in a long time. After you marry a demon and have his daughter, church takes on a new meaning.

"It's getting late, Mak. Head to your room, finish up your homework, then go to bed."

I waved off her huffy look and buried my face in my hands.

My head twinged once more before the migraine's fingers wrapped around my neck, pulling me down to darkness.

I knew my daughter could pick me up like I was a small doll. Blurry fireworks of pain-sound exploded behind my closed eyelids. My last conscious inhale burned with acrid brimstone.

Silence enveloped me as I crawled back through exhaustion. The stress of the day blanketed me like three comforters. Struggling for fresh air, I heard Ariel's concerned question.

"Three days?"

My room stopped spinning. Decorated with orange and white linens over solid red wood furnishings.

His presence warned some level of panic in my brain. Ignoring his fake relaxed stance leaning against my dresser, I left my room. It was morning; the smell of coffee reached me part-way down the stairs. My stomach growled.

"Hungry," he said in a liquid sex voice.

Damn, demon hearing.

"Stop it, you fucking prick," I said, aiming for the coffee pot.

He chuckled. "I'm not leaving, Raye. Screaming my name in morning orgasms doesn't make me want to leave, either."

"It wasn't your name." Belligerent and wrong, but I'm nothing if not stubborn.

"Really? Do you have a passionate crush on a mermaid?" His voice sounded smooth and sensual.

"You need to get out. I know you own the house. If you won't leave Makenna and I alone, we'll move out."

"I'm your protection."

"You're our biggest threat."

"Raye, I left because I didn't expect you to survive the birth. You're right about that. Also, if demons found out, they'd come for you. A human who can survive would be wanted as a breeder," he said, grinding his teeth.

"A breeding mare? I thought they wanted our daughter."

He shook his head.

"It's never been about protecting Makenna." He stopped as I took a step toward him. "Not completely. She's a demon. Her survival instinct gives her better odds."

He emphasized each word.

"Me? You left me to protect me? How many bad Lifetime movie marathons have you watched?" I snarked, afraid he may be telling me the truth. Although, the demons at the mall had attacked Mak. Or had they come after me and swarmed her when she'd defended me? My memories had been jumbled by fear and concern for my child.

He hung his head. "I'm never going to convince you it was in your best interest."

He pulled out the British accent he'd used to seduce me.

"Now you change accents?" I fumed.

"This is my natural accent, Raye. I spent five centuries in the United Kingdom before I met you and returned there when I left you. The tough-guy American accent was the one I put on to seduce you. Imagine my surprise to find you preferred my natural speaking voice. It's not a big deal in Europe."

Covering my face with the huge coffee cup I preferred, I let silence fill the room. If they were after me, why hadn't they come before? I asked Ariel when he started to twitch. Patience was a virtue he couldn't be bothered to wait for.

"Suspicions are not facts. They couldn't act until they knew Mak was demon. The little ambush at the mall was a test. Likely set up by the new Demon Lord, Kragen. The old one, Laythe, would've offered you protection and kept you safe."

"What happened to her?"

"Her mother beheaded her in front of Cim and Wretch."

I gasped. "She what?"

He waved it off like it was common. "She'd had it coming, not acting like a true demon. Not a vicious act toward others in decades. Obsidian had to put her down."

My knees tried to send my brain the message about losing balance by express. I realized it as I hit the floor, pain cascading down my body.

My coffee cup shattered, spraying my face and robe with sugary goodness. It was the last thing I remembered before passing out.

An empty lack of fear between regaining consciousness and remembering why I passed out wrapped me in a cloud of ignorance. Seconds later, a memory bitch-slapped and my heart thumped.

Trying to rise, I gasped in pain. "Mak."

"She's gone." A strange voice said with an odd touch of pity.

The sound made my stomach lurch.

My arms wouldn't move, neither would my legs. I was tied down. The blurriness in my vision started to fade as I frantically looked around.

Surrounded by a rolling cloth wall from old movies about third world hospitals, I saw a shadow standing on the other side. An IV pole stood next to me with clear fluid dripping and flowing into my arm. I wrinkled my nose at the smell of decay.

"What are you giving me? Where is my daughter?" I screamed, terrified now. My little girl was gone and I'd been taken, too. "Where the fuck is my miserable ex-husband? Did he put you up to this?"

If I ever saw Ariel again, I'd rip his damn dick off. I knew he could rebuild it with demon magic. As pissed as I was, I'd keep ripping 'em off until there wasn't enough flesh remaining for a beanie weenie.

"He's occupied."

The certainty made me queasy. Magic flowed from his words, slithering down my back.

A lump in my throat kept my scream internal and rattling inside my head.

"I've got you covered, my love. Just give me a minute." Ariel's voice sounded distant, an echo of the power it usually conveyed.

The shadow turned to the left. "You'll be dead shortly, Ariel, your wife and child not far behind."

The clipped, sure tone froze me. He had Makenna. Adrenaline gave me strength as I pulled at my bonds, tearing skin off. Wounds I could deal with later—I needed off this damn table. Yanking my right arm made the IV needle sting.

"You cannot get free."

The demon magic roiled through the curtain like a cloud of fog. Struggling to escape, I felt the flimsy cot creak beneath me. My body stopped responding as it hit me, my mind still screaming for my daughter and freedom. Visions of my daughter with this thing flashed through my mind.

Trying to push the images away, I looked around as I my body slid back down. I was in a warehouse; the ceiling was a good thirty feet up. I could see the ductwork. Leaning my head to the right, I checked out the floor. Polished concrete reflected the lights. Silence fell around me.

"Ariel?" I asked.

"Yes, love." He groaned with effort.

I wept. "They have her."

"I know." His voice cracked with fury and pain. "I offered myself in trade."

The shadow rippled. "I declined his offer."

It flowed through the wall and reformed into that of a demon standing over me.

He stood tall, close to six feet, if not more. Black, wavy hair fell over his shoulder from the ribbon at the back of his neck. His eyes were slitted, yellow, and fierce. He wore a three-piece suit, with a vest, a pocket watch, and white gloves. Hand on his hips, his expression bored. The polish on his shoes reflected the lights, making my eyes hurt.

"Raye, I'd introduce myself, but it's not important. You won't remember it." He reached over and placed a gloved hand on my mouth and nose.

Pushing my head back, I tried to pry his hand away. He didn't move. Instead, I braced myself and flung my right arm over my head. The IV burned as it fell away. Searching with one hand while consciousness ebbed from me, I found the needle and jammed it into his side. He pulled away and the motion spell on my body lifted. As I moved my legs to kick him, he spoke a few words and I slammed into the cart.

Darkness fell across my mind as tears ran down my cheeks. I'd never get to see my girl grow up, embarrass her in front of boyfriends, or cheer at her college graduation.

As I slipped away again, a rush of cold air hit my nose. There was a crash next to me. Guttural screams of rage followed by thumping punches.

Ariel's demon form rose above the barrier. Horns protruded from his hair, oily green scales covered his arms. He kicked down the cloth wall. Tufts of brown fur poked out of holes on his back, his feet clawed with talons. The other demon laid there, not fighting back, with a grin on his face. That's never good. Every bad guy in movies only does that if they're winning. A lesson Mak taught me during a horror movie marathon that ended with me behind the couch and her cheering like it was a sports event.

The two demons fought. It frightened and fascinated me. Each changed form so quickly, it looked like a special effects show. Only this one smelled of urine, blood, and acrid flop sweat.

"Ariel." Clearing my throat, I tried again. "Ariel."

It came out as a hoarse cry.

He turned his head to me and I gasped. His slitted eyes were furious, with blood coating the fangs exposed by his oversized grin. I'd slept with that thing, made love to him, fallen in love with him. Oh God, oh God, Makenna would look like that.

The shift back to his usual human form happened so fast I didn't see it. He stood up, leaving the bloodied beaten form on the floor. His last grin stuck in place. My ex-husband shifted his weight back and forth in the uncomfortable silence.

"Free me, you fucking prick," I said while he wallowed.

He let out a long breath. "You're welcome."

The slits opened on my wrists and ankles healed almost before he stood me up.

"What is in my IV?" I asked.

"You survived a demon birth, Raye."

"And? We've been over that before." Placing my hands on my hips, right where they liked to be when I interrogated our daughter, I stood my ground.

"They want you for breeding."

I swear he rolled his eyes.

I shivered. "He tried to kill me, Ari. How the hell am I supposed to give birth while dead?"

Ariel stared at me. I could see him thinking about telling me the truth. A look I'd trusted at one point made me squirm.

"You don't need to be alive, my love."

I tilted my head, aware I looked like a confused dog. "Excuse me?"

"Do you want the magic lesson now or on the way to rescue our daughter?"

A rip of pain was starting inside me. Gasping to keep it from running up my throat into my brain, I reached out and took Ariel's hand. "Where do we need to be?"

"We start at home."

Seconds later, we stood back in the house a few steps from where I'd fallen earlier. I wobbled. We'd vanished and appeared at the bottom of the stairs. Almost exactly where I'd fallen. I checked to make sure all my parts had made it, and that Ariel didn't reconstruct them with the curves he preferred on his mistresses.

"Good girl, she put up a fight," Ariel said from the hallway.

The wallpaper hung in threads down the staircase. Claw marks gouged the drywall underneath. The stairs had scratches on them three steps long and two inches deep.

"She made those?" I felt woozy.

He nodded. "The power of a demon with the compassion of a human. At least, I hope."

"Why do you hope?"

"How do you think she'd react to killing? Even another demon. She's still a child." He stormed up the stairs, yanking remnants of paper as he passed by.

Too much pain and terror rose up in me. My child was gone. Taken by a monster and there I stood, with another monster upstairs searching for clues. Crazy laughter rose up, threatening to turn me into a babbling, cackling lunatic.

As Ariel thumped around, I fought to get a grip. Forcing my breathing back to normal, I felt fury rise inside of me. Burning fury filled every ounce of my being, sweat popping up on my forehead.

I'd rip the head off whoever took my baby girl. I didn't care she'd turn into a monster—I loved her unconditionally and would kill to get her back.

Years of surety that Ariel would never defend us, if needed, set aside as his angry shouts fell from upstairs. His appearance now, just before she'd been taken, couldn't be a coincidence. Either he'd been telling the truth when he said he'd left for our protection, or he'd guided his enemies to us with this visit.

Either way, I needed him right now. I'd never felt inadequate as a parent before, even when the shifting began. Makenna's growth was normal until she turned twelve. No changing into strange things or bizarre voices, any of the horror movie fears I'd had early on.

The two of us got along well. I'd told her about her father when she was ten. I figured with puberty coming up soon, I'd rather be ahead of that problem.

She took it well, considering. The nightmares ended after a month and she'd stopped asking me if she was going to be a freak. We'd fought over curfew when the first shift happened.

Had that really been seven months ago? Makenna had stomped up the stairs to tell me how unfair I was, entering my room with goat slitted eyes, horns, and a gravelly voice. The color had drained from my face and it'd taken her a minute to notice I'd gone silent.

Her reaction to herself in the mirror still broke my heart. "I'm ugly, Mom. How could you do this to me? What were you thinking? How could you not know he was a demon?"

The melodrama of a teen in demon form reflected in the mirror gave me tremors. I'd hidden them the best I could.

I'd told her she was my daughter and I loved her. She'd shifted back to my little girl while crying on my shoulder. I hoped she didn't hear me wake frightened for weeks afterwards.

"Fuck, fuck, fuck," Ariel shouted, bounding down the stairs. "I can't find a clue."

"Who was the man torturing me?" I asked. "Maybe he has something to do with it."

His labored sigh aggravated me. "He's an assassin for hire."

"So, anyone you pissed off in four or five decades could have our daughter?"

"Four or five centuries. And yes." The answer felt so casual, it stung.

Running my hand through my hair, I sniffed. "I stink. Horribly. When this is over, I'm taking a bath for a week."

"You can bathe now, I'll make calls. It's better I found out which of my enemies is in town than for us to run around where we can get picked up again."

The control I'd imposed started to slip away as my palms went clammy. "Here?"

Fear flashed in his eyes. It didn't fit him.

"We're going to find her, Raye. If I have to rip apart every demon in town."

The fierce anger in his voice made me wince. He meant it. Well, it's about freaking time. If I'd said it out loud, another fight would've delayed us.

"I'll clean up. There's camping gear in the hallway closet, Ari."

"What do we need that for?" he asked.

"Flashlights, compass, in case we have to go looking outside of town." My stomach twisted as I spoke.

Working in the emergency room, I'd heard so many stories of missing people. Each time, the doctors noted how easy it was to vanish in the swamps down river. You could be two hundred yards from civilization and no one would see you.

Running up the stairs, I mentally catalogued all of the places my family used to fish. Miles of swamp south of New Orleans hid small outcroppings of land large enough for fishing cabins. At that point, I'd wished I'd put a tracking device in her arm. Overbearing, yes. Necessary, fuck yeah.

Chapter Four

Following my former husband through the swamp, I noted a few things I'd missed before. His enhanced senses included the ability to hear crocodiles swimming toward us. The smells overwhelmed me. I'd thrown up twice by the time we found signs of a struggle.

The inhuman way Ariel moved struck me. His neck twisted like an insect's. I'd figured even a demon would move their limbs like a human. He'd lengthened his feet and arms with a thought, moving faster than I could in a truck.

Desire rose in me that had nothing to do with passion. "Whammy me again and I'll shoot you."

He laughed, cold and distant. I considered shooting him. Angry tears flowed over my cheeks. Mak had been gone for hours. She'd never spent a night away from home. I'd feared she'd shift and be killed by the other child's parents.

I had no idea how Ariel took the stench. Then again, I wondered if his natural body odor ranked in line with hot, summer swamp. If they made that into a cologne for demons, women like me wouldn't hook up with 'em. I don't care how sexy you are; if you stink, I'm not getting sweaty with you.

Blowing another stray hair out of my face, I stared at his back, whispering, "See anything?"

He shot me the bird with a foot-long finger.

"Fuck you, demon."

His back shook with laughter. "Mak knows this area. She's left claw marks on trees along the shore."

We'd camped out here a couple of times when I'd taught her how to hunt. "I don't see any marks."

"They didn't walk through the water. The trail." He nodded at the water's edge. "Made it easier to carry her. She marked every tree for a mile."

Glaring at the place he indicated, I couldn't see anything. "Where?"

"You have to know what you're looking for," he said.

Sighing, I trotted along behind him. "My father would be proud. We finally took this damn waders out of the box."

He'd been so happy when I got married. Worried about his only child, he'd welcomed Ariel to the family with hunting and fishing trips. He'd passed away before he could find out Ari'd been hunting wild game for centuries.

"He was a good man." Ariel turned around, pulling me into a kiss.

I struggled, mumbling against his mouth. "What are you doing?"

I heard voices. A trembling voice said, "Never mind, it's a couple fishing together. Ick, did you see them kiss? What's up with humans?"

A low male rumble gave me the impression of a large-chested man. "They have sex, that's why they have children, you moron. No one is coming for the girl. Obsidian wants her alive but that doesn't mean we can't mess her up. Send the pictures to her dad's cell phone. He'll get away from Smith soon enough."

Ariel's fingers dug into my back. I hadn't seen him move. I bit my tongue to keep from crying out.

The other voice, sounding more afraid, said, "The sooner we get the girl to Thailand, the faster we get out of our contract to that bitch. She scares me."

There was a deep laugh. "She's in town. Watch how you speak of her."

Ariel's breath came in gasps. I'd heard the name before, something Mak had said after a training session with Wretch. I knew it wasn't good if he'd told Mak to fear her.

Ariel murmured, "At least we know who and why."

I saw the backs of the demons as they retreated down the pathway. "Why?"

"I broke into her lab last year. She's doing bizarre experiments, trying to create demons from shifters. It's left a trail of half-demons running around slaughtering people. There was a mass killing in Canada, an entire pack of werewolves torn to pieces." His face contorted with what I assumed was disgust.

I thought about mentioning his ease at combining human and demon but my fear for my daughter came first. "We can go now."

"No, we can't. They won't buy us being innocent. They'll stand back thirty or forty yards and wait."

"What do we do? They have her." Keeping terror from my voice took effort.

"We know where they are now," he said.

The smell of decaying flesh hit me and the bottom of my stomach dropped out.

"Mak," I whispered in terror.

"Not her, prey animal." Ariel ground out. "What do you eat?"

"Food." I wobbled a bit as he picked me up.

He grunted. "I'm either going to drop you and leave you or cover you with my body until you moan."

That shouldn't have made me gasp. Clamping down on my tongue, I hoped I covered the rush of passion I felt. "Get our daughter home safe, demon."

"Agreed."

We made it back to the place where we entered the meandering river. He placed me on the dry ground, jumping up before a huge set of jaws clamped down on his right ankle. He winced in pain as I stood in shock.

Raising a rambunctious child prepared me for sudden panicked rescue. Makenna once got her head stuck in the steel bars at the school. As her head turned red, I'd run to the grounds keeper at the far end with the chainsaw.

Pulling the knife from my belt, I leaned forward with my left hand on Ariel's hip to keep from losing ground. The crocodile started to twist as the underside of his head became visible with a crunch of bones. I slashed his throat open. Blood sprayed, sticking to my face as I stabbed again at the softer flesh.

Ariel dropped to his left knee, angling to get the jaws, now held by an angry beast, in his hands. He shifted into a demon form with claws six inches long. With one yank, he removed the skin I'd flayed, jamming a claw inside. Gagging from the stench, I backed up a few steps, eyeing the way we came. To get caught would doom my daughter.

"Enough," I screamed. The gun I'd tucked into my waders fit my hand perfectly. It took two shots before the animal let go.

Ariel turned to me in slow, dangerous fury. "You could have shot me."

This time, he didn't bother to shift back to human.

"I've been to the gun range, I hit the target every time. If I shoot you, I'll aim for your neck with bigger ammo."

"Decapitation by gunfire?" His expression looked wary and somewhat impressed.

Sighing, I explained. "Buckshot, or hand grenade would work."

He stood, turning his foot back and forth as he shifted to human form. Clothed, I couldn't tell if there was a wound through the magically created clothing.

"You've practiced killing demons?" His brows furrowed.

I forced a grin, knowing it looked hostile. "I used our wedding photo for target practice."

I'd never imagined he'd pale in front of me. "I didn't know."

"Of course not, you'd have to be here." Stomping off in hip waders with blood spatter felt like the perfect flourish.

Hearing his delighted laughter behind me was not the desired response, but I found myself smiling. Mak had one hell of a rescue coming.

The truck we'd rented in the color of primer and camouflage stood on blocks. The tires were missing, the guns we'd left in the rack were gone, and someone had painted 'Tough shit losers' on the hood.

"Demons," Ariel said.

"No, kids." I corrected. "Unless you have demons who act like stupid teenagers, this is just a prank by local hunters. We're barely three hundred yards from the road and with the prevalence of cell phones, the thought they'd actually strand people wouldn't occur to them."

"Can I kill them?"

My breath caught in my throat. "Kill children for a prank? Fuck, no."

"Scare them." He shifted into demon form complete with fleshy pink wings and hooves. The bat-like face sniffed the air, fixed on a scent, and took flight.

I checked the glove box and found more ammunition for the gun. Screams of terror filled the air. The sound of ATVs revving up came closer. I could make out shouts of 'It's the Devil' and 'I swear I didn't get her pregnant.'

Well, that kid had some penance coming to him. I held the loaded gun, safety engaged, in front of me as two boys in their late teens or early twenties burst through the edge of the clearing at top speed. Each machine had two tires loaded on the back. It may be the only reason they didn't flip as they noticed me and jerked the steering wheels.

"Holy hell, you bitch! Do you work with the devil?" one of the boys asked me. Frightened tears glistened on his cheeks.

"The tires," I said.

The other boy shook so hard I could hear the machine rattling.

I nodded at him. "Turn those off, put the tires back on my truck."

The smell of sweat, urine, and fear smacked me as they rushed to obey.

"I can't believe you sent him after us," one of them said, glaring at me.

"Sent who?" I asked.

Ariel walked back into the clearing in the fishing outfit he'd had on earlier. "Honey, I couldn't find the monster, but I damn near died when two kids came flying past me."

He'd laid on the southern accent.

It didn't quite fit but the boys were too frightened to notice.

One of the young men, who looked older close up, turned and his jaw dropped open. "Mister, it didn't get you?"

He shook his head. "No, son. I heard your screams but didn't see anything. Are you sure there was something up there?" He glared at all three of us. "I want a good answer or my wife shoots you for stealing and trying to run me over."

Payback for the target practice remark, I was sure. Fighting the urge to smile, I answered, "I didn't see anything. These two did fly out of the woods like they were being chased. Think it went into the water?"

It took a moment before Ariel caught where I was going. These two had guns and could distract the demons with Makenna. Chaos and mayhem would be a great cover for a rescue.

The hunters stood up, puffing out their chests like they hadn't peed themselves moments earlier.

They looked alike in their camouflage coveralls, each about average height with brown hair poking out of baseball caps, also in the camo motif. They could've been brothers or cousins with short beards, cheeks full of tobacco, and tanned skin.

Ariel walked over to me, wrapping me in a hug. "Thanks, love. I'll check their machines."

The boys hung their heads as Ari ruffled through their packs pulling out our identification, items from the glove box, and extra ammunition I'd packed to take out the demons.

"Looks like you didn't come out here prepared," I said to the tops of their heads.

They were fascinated with the ground.

"Boys? Do you want to apologize for robbing us?" I clicked the gun with a fingernail.

Nerves so raw on them, they jumped at the noise.

"We're sorry, ma'am, sir." Their voices squeaked with puberty.

"Maybe the monster you saw took off through the swampy river over there." I gestured with the gun back the way we'd come. "You can take off to find it. Holler loud enough for us to hear you, and we might show up to help."

Fierce gray eyes met mine. "It's our kill."

Suppressing a smile, I replied, "Yes, son."

The boys hopped on their machines, taking off at a reckless speed.

Ariel laughed until he had to sit down. "You just fed those two to demons. You are more like me than you realize."

"I'm hoping they distract them long enough for us to get Makenna. Now, get your sick ass into the truck. I want to drive as far as we can in case we need an engine-powered escape."

He stood up, eyeing me with a smile. "Yes, ma'am."

"Don't mock those boys. They could've killed you, Ari."

"I noticed how you didn't check to see if I was okay," he complained.

Starting the truck, I stared at him. "You fly around looking like a demon and a human will shoot your ass out of the sky. I might feel a momentary pang, but you'd be asking for it."

He shifted his gaze out the window. "You sent those boys to their death."

"No, I didn't. They'll get out of our sight and run. One of them needs to change his underwear."

"You can't be sure, Raye."

"Yes, I can. Hear that?" I stopped the truck at the edge of the clearing. The small engines of their ATVs roared in the distance, heading the opposite direction from trouble.

Ariel looked confused. "But they wanted to kill something."

"Small, furry, and cute. They aren't going to hunt a creature who can fight back."

Which was why I hated hunting. I understood the need to pack your freezer for the year. Hell, I'd considered it. But I couldn't kill the animals myself. I bought mine at the store.

Driving around the swamp was stupid. The tires got stuck three times. I'd bounced off two trees that'd looked small enough to break. Leaving the truck behind, we walked the last twenty minutes, careful to stay on dry ground and away from water deep enough to hide more crocodiles.

"I hate you," I said to Ariel.

"Well, that took a while." He brushed it off.

Trying to build fury toward him, I found it sputtering out. I'd always been able to build up a head of full anger when I thought of him. "You aren't taking me seriously."

He stopped, holding a branch to keep it from snapping me in the face as I followed him. "You said it on our wedding night."

Whoa, I'd forgotten about that. "I didn't mean it then."

He cut his blue eyes at me. Silky black locks snuck out of his hat, sweat sticking to his neck. He looked like a cover model.

"And now?" His voice felt like melted chocolate.

Apparently, I needed sugar. "I mean it."

"Your eyes say differently."

I blinked. "I haven't been laid in years. That's lust, not love."

"They're related, Raye."

My turn to glare. "You proved you could sleep with an entire hospital of nurses."

"Ten, Raye, is not an entire hospital."

He sounded exasperated, like we'd had this fight a dozen times, which we had.

In the four years of our custody battle, I'd accused him of sleeping with everyone but the judge. I'd have done that except I knew her wife.

"It was everyone in the ER, where I worked." I found my ability to scream at him comforting.

"Your boss punched me in the nuts." He winced with the memory.

I laughed. "She's gay. You have the wrong parts."

"I can change."

Another visual I'd need a bottle of tequila to erase. "Ari, that doesn't work. She likes women, not male demons who can fake it."

He sighed, stripping his shirt off. Perfect abs glistened with sweat. Wiping down with the balled up shirt, he smirked at the attention.

"Still like this?" He gestured to his body.

"If that was your only form, yes." A shiver ran down my spine. "The demon look you sport makes me vomit."

It hurt him. I knew shredding his ego was a bitch move, especially in light of what we were doing. So, I'm not a perfect ex-wife.

Sighing, he crouched down, waving his arm behind him for me to do the same.

"Are we close?" I asked in a stage whisper.

The response came from the low-voiced demon. "Someone is here. Go hunting."

Choking back fear, I grabbed Ariel's belt loops. "Don't you run off on me."

Instead, he pulled me under him. Wriggling under his body got an expected reaction. He winked at me right before shifting into a crocodile. I screamed. In my head, I knew it was Ariel, yet a two-hundred-pound, scaly croc lay on top of me, wiggling and smiling. I was so scared. I fought to keep from vomiting on myself. There was a rumbling in the stomach laid on mine and I'd bet he was laughing.

"You prick. They can see me," I said.

He opened massive jaws, leaning down to me. I gagged, turning my face away and holding up an arm. Which he bit.

"You leave a mark on me and I'm getting a full body makeover at your expense."

There was that rumbling feeling again.

Boots ran past me.

"Crocodile," a demon squeaked.

"Keep looking." It was an order.

"Wait," Boots gasped. "The croc has a woman pinned. Can I watch?"

"Fucking sicko," I whispered through gritted teeth.

Another set of boots, these larger with steel toes, passed by. "As much fun as that would be," he said. "We have a demon to string up."

Ariel picked that moment to step on my knee with a back leg. I grunted, trying to flip him over. His jaws pulled my arm across my face, twisting me at the middle.

"You're saving my life and I'm going to thank you for it later." I paused as his jaws eased up. "With words, you pervert."

The hair on the back of my neck stood up. Fighting not to look over my shoulder, I must've looked different because Ariel made a guttural sound in his throat, gullet? No, throat, and took off running. Afraid to look up and see demons holding a gun to my head, I rolled over to my stomach, clutching the arm he'd held in his jaws. Blood soaked my sleeve.

I was not cut out for this. I could handle an entire emergency room after a fifty-car pile up on the highway. This was different. Inhuman smells filled my lungs, gagging me. Curling my legs under me, my knee gave out. Fighting back pain that ran up my legs to my back, I crawled to a tree.

My daughter needed me, I kept repeating to myself as I fought waves of nausea and pain. A demon grinned ten yards away. In his current form, I couldn't tell if it was Ariel or one of the others. Since demons clothing was magic, there weren't any clothes on the ground near the creature to give me a clue.

I'm not sure it would have mattered. The fear and pain joined up in my chest as I screamed in terror. "Give me back my daughter."

He blinked. "You want her? Come get her."

The demon flapped its wings, filling the air with the horrid smell of decay as it took off.

Stumbling from tree to tree, I lost him after only a few steps. "Makenna, I'm so sorry. I can't get to you."

The tears flowed down my face, blurring my vision. Pain, horrible tearing, ripping, soul-wrenching pain burned inside my chest. "I love you, my baby girl."

Something smacked into my back, knocking me down in the dirt. I barely pushed my hands down to get my nostrils free when the demons claws landed on either side of my head.

"I'll make you beg for her life, then kill her." It was the squeaky demon.

Thunder rumbled in front of me. A demon claw twisted as the creature turned. I felt the ground tremble as hooves, shrouded in dust and covered in swamp muck, appeared a short distance away. Fear stilled my movements. Not knowing which, if any, was Ariel kept me thinking. If these two, whoever they were, would get into a fight, I might make the bushes on my left. I got my wish.

"You fuck up, why are you chasing her? She's injured. We can pull her apart later. Get back to the girl, her father is around here." His deep voice rattled around the trees.

"You promised me I could play with his wife. I never offered to babysit."

A stench that had to be nervous demon sweat gagged me.

Rolling to my side, I saw the squeaky demon turn away from me, flexing his wings in anger. It concealed me from the other demon stomping his hooves in what looked, from what little I could see, like a centaur.

If Ariel told me those didn't exist, it was only demons playing games with humans, I'd kick him. I needed some of my childhood fairy tale creatures to be real.

The smaller, squeakier demon hopped off me and before I could blink, they'd started arguing a few yards away. I pulled my knees to my chest. The wounded one screamed in a slightly quieter voice this time. Rocking back and forth on my ass, I managed to get both feet under me while leaning to grab a tree.

The demons couldn't decide who would eat me first, and not in the good way. I pulled painkillers out of my pocket, downed them with the bottle of water Ariel forced me to tie to my belt, and then bolted. I limped every other step until the pain was so bad it didn't matter how I compensated for it.

"You bitch, I'll kill you," a demon yelled behind me. Hooves smacked against the ground.

"Makenna," I screamed. "Where are you?"

They knew where I was—might as well make a ton of noise.

"Help me! There are two men trying to steal the deer I killed," I hollered toward the river, hoping hunters would hear me.

"Mom." Makenna's frightened voice shattered my heart. "They tied me up, I can't move."

"Your dad's here somewhere, keep yelling, I've got the bastards chasing me," I yelled back.

"Son of a bitch." The deep voice felt too close. "We've left the girl unguarded. Go get her."

The other demon refused. "I get the woman. You promised."

"Are you pouting? Son, I'm going to rip your wings off myself. Obsidian sent us to punish Ariel. Once we kill his daughter, while he watches, we can chase down the breeding bitch. Maybe, I can make a son who doesn't whine."

Well, seems the demon community could use a good therapist. I didn't slow down but had to decide—do I run toward my daughter, bringing the demons with me, or away from her voice to give Ariel a chance at rescuing her?

My daughter's safety took precedence and I turned back toward the clearing where we'd left the truck.

I didn't know I could move that fast. I stumbled twice when my knee tried to give out. The edge of the clearing came into view and I jumped forward. As I braced myself to land, my ankles were caught in a vise grip and yanked into the air. I smacked into a tree with my face.

Blood ran into my nose, making me breathe through my mouth. "Great."

The demon son stared at me from demon eyes. "It looks like Father and I are going to keep you for breeding."

I swear I heard an engine starting up. "Your mother would love that."

"I ripped my mother's body to pieces when I was born, as your daughter should have done to you." He smacked my ass.

"Pervert."

"Nice jiggle." His voice thickened with passion.

"Oh no, you don't. I got fixed after my daughter was born, you can't get me pregnant." It was a lie, of sorts. The damage to my system prevented me from conceiving again. Until today, I'd cursed it.

He twisted me around to face him.

Demon faces disgust me. Upside down, when I could see up its bat-like nose, I had a simple reaction. I barfed on him.

He laughed. "That doesn't bother me."

"Because it smells better than you," I spat back at him, feeling dizzy.

Blood oozed in chest wounds moments before the sound of the gunshots reached my ears. The demon jammed my feet into tree branches and fled.

I couldn't see and rocking back and forth to try to grab the tree made me vomit again. "Drop me, or they'll shoot again."

I'd hoped it was the hunters we ran into earlier. Teen boys didn't stand a chance against demons, but well-armed teen boys with ATV's could get away.

"Sorry, ma'am. It seems we found the creature. Hold on, we'll get you down." The panicked boy from earlier came into sight, white as snow, his rifle shaking in his hand. Terrified or not, years of practice wouldn't allow him to miss by much.

I smashed into the ground hearing a barrage of gun shots.

"We have to go. Mom will kill us if we aren't home by dinner. We can call the cops on the way."

A threat from Mom was enough for the brother to drop me. I heard more shots as their tires vanished in the distance.

"Get up, bitch." The father demon kicked my ribs.

Pain lanced through my system. I'd pass out from it soon. The demon wrapped an arm around my waist. I gagged and dry-heaved while he carried me.

I couldn't fight. My head bobbed along, increasing the feeling of being woozy. Trees blurred by.

"Mom, Dad's unconscious," Makenna screamed.

Shit, the rescue was up to me, then. I let my body go limp, pretending to pass out so I could conserve my energy. I needed a plan.

Mak needed me. Breathing slowly, I took inventory of what I had on me. There was a bowie knife in one of my boots, a small handgun in the other... damn, I'd forgotten about that. First aid kit, small, tucked inside the hunting vest, and three fishing lines with hooks already attached. Glued, in fact—I hated tying them on.

The gun sat against my calf on the damaged leg.

"Son," the older demon yelled. "Get your horny ass over here. We have work to do."

We rounded a group of trees and there hung Makenna. Tied up in a square cage, her wrists and ankles handcuffed to the corners. I caught her eye and winked at her.

She tried to smile at me but I could see the tear tracks left on her face, her bloodied lip, and bruises along her arms. My girl had fought back.

Glancing around, I found Ariel. He'd changed back to his human form and lay under Mak's cage.

Blood pooled thickly under his head. One arm looked clearly broken in two, skin about to snap between the pieces. As I watched, the skin grew over the exposed bone.

He was healing? Holy shit, he was alive and healing. We might have a chance. I couldn't get his attention before the demon carrying me threw me into a tent. I didn't move even when my arms, trapped under me, kept me from brushing off his curious hands.

"Baby, I'm going to make you scream for me, then beg for your life." His fingers tingled along the inside of my thighs.

Damn, demon magic. Repulsive, yet able to make a woman's body yearn for them. Closing my eyes, I forced the image of him as a bat-winged thing into my vision. The desire ebbed.

"Take your hands out of her crotch. First, we kill the kid." His father's earlier anger ebbed into exasperation.

The abomination huffed out a foul breath before leaving me alone in the tent.

I moved my head to peer out of the opening. Ariel winked at me.

"Mom, I'm fine." Mak announced defiantly.

Wriggling to the tent opening, I saw the demons circling below her like sharks ready to feed.

"What do you want with my daughter?" I screamed, trying to delay their plans.

The abomination laughed. "We need breeders. Might even keep you alive if you're good to me."

Failing to fight the gag reflex, I bent my head forward to make it look like a cough. There was nothing left in my stomach. Mak's growl brought me up straight. The father demon stood tall enough to look her in the eyes. He grabbed the side of the cage.

She slid toward him with fear in her eyes. "Leave me alone, your pervert. Are you listed on the sexual predator list? I could call it in for you."

"Mak." I choked on panic.

Crawling out of the tent, I saw Ariel start to move. We needed to get her down and kill two demons without any help.

What would Lara Croft do? I know I didn't speak the words aloud, and yet, I had three demons staring at me with amusement.

Well, I did know what kept demons' attention. Struggling to my feet, I stripped. The bruises from my knee bled to the gator print on my calf. The entire thing was purple. At least, there wasn't any broken skin.

My arm had puncture wounds weeping in a semicircle. I ignored it. Across a clearing sat my daughter, chained to a cage behind two demons who'd kill her.

My daughter and her father laughed as I ran naked across the field at her stunned captors. Ariel's wounds appeared healed as I limped toward the pedophile groping the cage for my daughter's girly parts.

"Leave her alone," I yelled, moving fast. "I'll kick your nuts into your stomach."

He barely paid attention. "I'm a demon. They'll drop back down before I crush your skull."

"A few minutes ago, you were keeping me alive." I copied the baseball slide I'd seen on TV, aiming for his knees.

"That was when I liked you." His previous squeaky tone was replaced by cold fury.

"Fickle bitch." I kicked him with both legs and my full weight.

His bones cracked, bending his knee outward. With a wiggle of his leg, he resumed frightening my child.

"Mom," Makenna screamed. "He's going to rape me."

That word—every woman knows that word and the terror it instills.

"No fucking way." Ariel appeared above me. "Let go of my daughter."

I wobbled to my feet, covered in scrapes and grass. The other demon's body lay a few feet away, dissolving into dust. Maybe we could do this; only the son demon to go.

Stumbling back to the tent, I picked up a gun I'd seen when getting out of my clothes. Returning to Ariel's side, I pointed it at the demon's temple. He had to be a foot taller than me, so a few steps back worked well. Mak's whimpering cries drove me to push the barrel against his head and flipping off the safety.

"You don't mess with my family."

The demon turned his head toward me. "What are you doing?"

"Protecting my child, you fucking prick." I pulled the trigger.

A hole appeared in the side of his head, knocking him sideways.

"Why?" He sounded genuinely surprised.

Ariel watched him fall. "Demons don't take care of their children. That protective instinct humans have, especially mothers, doesn't exist. I told you we aren't nice."

"That's messed up," Mak said through tears.

"Watch your language," Ariel and I said at the same time.

She rolled her eyes at me and it made me happy.

The demon grabbed Ariel around the throat, lifting him off the ground.

Mak screamed, "Mom, save him."

I fumbled with the strange gun, unable to get another round to load. "Dammit."

Then, my child changed. Her human form shifted into a worm, pulling free of the restraints she'd obviously been able to get out of all along—we'd talk about that later—then into a scorpion. Turning her claw sideways, she slipped it between the bars aiming for the demon's neck.

He pushed Ariel in her path before she could react. Gashes appeared on his neck as she yanked her claw away.

"Sorry, Dad." She turned into a snake, sliding out of the cage and around the demon's legs.

I heard the crunch right before his leg gave out. Ariel dropped to the ground in a crouch. He shifted into a mountain lion as he hit. Makenna didn't let up, still squeezing.

The demon shifted into a huge worm, falling over and slithering away from my daughter. Mak changed into her human form, scrambling over to me. We helped each other to the tent.

"We need clothes." I threw things around.

"Mom, he could die." She tried to get away.

"He's been fighting other demons for centuries. He'll win. If not, his enemies won't come after us again." Cold, yeah, but I had good reason.

She nodded weakly, tears flowing down her beautiful face. Thin and fragile, she began to mourn a man who was still alive and hadn't been around for most of a decade. I placed her at the opening of the tent, reaching in to get my clothes. When I stepped back out, she'd spoken the spell Wretch had taught her to cover herself. It was the one spell she knew I wanted. She could do the same to me, but it felt odd not to have actual material on my body.

My clothes wouldn't go on. Instead, Mak dressed me in cargo pants and a large t-shirt. Her first sob ripped at me.

"Son of a bitch," I growled, pushing her into the tent. "Stay there."

Making my way back to the gun hurt. Pain shot up my leg and yanked at my head. Ariel was winning the fight, for what I could see. I needed to guarantee it or my daughter wouldn't forgive me.

"Let go of my husband, you prick." I aimed the gun.

The demon turned to me and I shivered. The barrel wobbled more toward Ariel's head.

Brittle laughter came from its throat. "We are only at the beginning."

I blew its head off. "Bring it."

Ariel caught me right before I hit the ground. In moments, we were back at home. Mak rushed to me, hugging me so hard it hurt. I didn't say a word, reveling in her love.

"I'll always get you, no matter what your father's enemies throw at me." I kissed her head.

She mumbled into my shirt. "You turned into a badass today, Mom."

"Yes, she did." He sounded impressed. "Remind me never to leave you armed."

That struck something in Mak. Not me, this time.

She whirled on him. "You never should have left, ever. You get that now, right? I can protect Mom. You need to go. Hunt down whoever wants to keep my mother. That is the only way we'll be safe."

"Bright girl." He bowed. "I shall leave you to recover while I hunt my enemies. There's a spell on my death. If I die, you'll get notice within moments. Mak." He turned to her. "You'll feel it. I've provided for both of you, all of my belongings and holdings become yours upon my death."

"I only want Mom."

I sniffled. "That's my girl."

"I have seventeen homes around the world. You will be safe in any of them." He vanished.

"Hell of an exit line." She wiped tears from her face.

"Yeah, he'll be back. He always comes back." I knew the truth in the words as I spoke.

Chapter Five

Standing in the doorway felt like an intrusion. Makenna's fists moved so fast I barely had time to notice before she hit the punching bag. Heavy bag, that's what Wretch called it. He looked like a well-trained martial artist at the moment; usually, he gave off a slimy vibe. Not the bad guy kind, but the one all women know from the slick dude at the end of the bar who bathed in awful cologne and dressed in leisure suits with furry chests.

The light from the door behind me vanished as someone entered. Turning, I saw Cimmerian. They called him the Death Dealer, Dragon Lord of the Arcane Court. He had a body mortal men dreamed about and he didn't care. His green eyes flicked down to me, the smile lines on his face deepening. The expression looked odd on his face.

He was tall, two heads over me tall. I stepped aside to let him into the room. Within three steps, a dragon stood there unfolding his wings, his head brushing the ceiling.

My daughter gasped, running to him, hugging his scaly middle.

"Nice to see you, too, little one," he rasped.

"Let go of the nice dragon, Mak. You're hurting him."

He genuinely laughed at me. "I sound gravelly after a change. She cannot hurt me."

It was the truth. I knew it, and so did my daughter.

"Mom, he's a dragon. He'll be fine." Rolling her eyes at me, she went back to punching.

A blur later, Cimmerian, the man, stood in front of me. "She needs to know shifting rapidly, and often, is common."

Nodding, I tried to understand. This was our new life—training, avoiding Ariel's enemies, and more training. To be by my daughter's side, I'd fight the devil himself.